Cinderella

THE PLAY

FEATURING:

The Stepmother

ALSO STARRING:

Cinderella
Stepsister
Prince
Narrator

Adapted by Nora Gaydos
Illustrated by Barbara Vagnozzi

Narrator

Once upon a time, there lived a nice girl named Cinderella. She lived with her mean stepmother and her mean stepsister.

Stepmother

Make the beds and mop the floors, Cinderella!

Stepsister

Scrub the tub and clean the plates, Cinderella!

Narrator

All day and night, Cinderella had to clean and mop and scrub the house. But she did it with a smile on her face.

Cinderella

One day, I will leave this house, and I will be happy all the time.

Narrator

Knock, knock, knock. A man was at the door with a note.

Stepmother

Look! The king wants all the girls in the land to come to a ball at the castle.

Stepsister

And the prince will pick one girl to be his wife! Oh, Mother, it just has to be me!

Cinderella

Or maybe it will be me! Yes, yes! I need to make a dress— and fast.

Stepmother

Stop, Cinderella! You will not go to the ball until you do all of your jobs.

Cinderella

But I just cleaned the whole house!

Stepsister

Well, now you need to fix my dress, brush my hair, shine my shoes, and clean the house . . . again!

4

Narrator

After doing all of her jobs, Cinderella had no time to make a dress for herself.

Stepmother

It is time for the ball, Cinderella. Too bad you have to stay home.

Stepsister

How sad for Cinderella. She will not get to meet the prince.

Cinderella

One day, I will meet the prince. I will, I will, I will!

Narrator

Just then, there was a puff of smoke.

Cinderella

Who are you?

Narrator

It was Cinderella's fairy godmother. She asked Cinderella why she looked so sad.

Cinderella

The king wants all the girls in the land to meet the prince, but I can't go to the ball like this.

Narrator

So the fairy godmother waved her magic wand, and *poof* . . . Cinderella had a pink silk dress and fine glass slippers.

Cinderella

Wow! Look at me! Thank you, fairy godmother. Can I go to meet the prince now?

Narrator

The fairy godmother told Cinderella that she had to leave the ball before the clock struck 12:00. She told her to

Narrator

say some magic words, and Cinderella did.

Cinderella

One and two and three and four—I am at the castle door!

Narrator

Poof! Cinderella stepped into the castle. The prince looked at Cinderella, and Cinderella looked at the prince.

Stepsister

Who is that girl?

Stepmother

And where did she get such a fine pink dress?

Prince

Oh, my! Who is that girl? I will ask her to dance with me.

Narrator

The prince and Cinderella danced together all night long. Then, the clock started to chime. It was 12:00.

Cinderella

Oh, no, I have to go!

Prince

Please don't go! Please stay with me.

Cinderella

No, no! I have to go!

Narrator

Cinderella ran down the steps, but she lost one of her glass slippers.

Prince

I have to find the girl who lost this slipper. I want her to be my wife!

Narrator

The next day, the prince went to every house in the land.

Prince

I must find the girl who lost this slipper!

Narrator

Finally, the prince knocked on the door of Cinderella's house.

Stepsister

Oh, my, the prince is here!

Prince

Good day. I am the prince. I am here to find the girl who lost this glass slipper.

Stepsister

That is MY glass slipper! It will fit me. You will see!

Narrator

So the prince tried to put the slipper on her very big foot.

Stepmother

Oh, no! Let me help! You have to get your foot into that slipper!

Cinderella

May I try the glass slipper on my foot?

Prince

Who are you?

Stepsister

That is Cinderella. She just cleans the house!

Stepmother

Go away, Cinderella. Go to your room!

Prince

No. Please stay and try the slipper on your foot.

Narrator

So the prince got on his knees and slid the slipper onto Cinderella's foot.

Prince

It fits! You are the girl from the ball!

Stepsister

Oh, Mother, she was the girl who danced with the prince!

Stepmother

NOOOOOOOOOOOO! This cannot be true!

Prince

Will you come to the castle and be my wife?

Cinderella

Yes, I will!

Narrator

And from that time on, Cinderella and the prince lived happily ever after . . . and the mean stepmother and stepsister had to clean and scrub the house all by themselves!

Cinderella
THE PLAY

FEATURING:

The Stepsister

ALSO STARRING:

Stepmother
Cinderella
Prince
Narrator

Adapted by Nora Gaydos
Illustrated by Barbara Vagnozzi

Narrator

Once upon a time, there lived a nice girl named Cinderella. She lived with her mean stepmother and her mean stepsister.

Stepmother

Make the beds and mop the floors, Cinderella!

Stepsister

Scrub the tub and clean the plates, Cinderella!

Narrator

All day and night, Cinderella had to clean and mop and scrub the house. But she did it with a smile on her face.

Cinderella

One day, I will leave this house, and I will be happy all the time.

Narrator

Knock, knock, knock. A man was at the door with a note.

Stepmother

Look! The king wants all the girls in the land to come to a ball at the castle.

Stepsister

And the prince will pick one girl to be his wife! Oh, Mother, it just has to be me!

Cinderella

Or maybe it will be me! Yes, yes! I need to make a dress—and fast.

Stepmother

Stop, Cinderella! You will not go to the ball until you do all of your jobs.

Cinderella

But I just cleaned the whole house!

Stepsister

Well, now you need to fix my dress, brush my hair, shine my shoes, and clean the house . . . again!

4

Narrator

After doing all of her jobs, Cinderella had no time to make a dress for herself.

Stepmother

It is time for the ball, Cinderella. Too bad you have to stay home.

Stepsister

How sad for Cinderella. She will not get to meet the prince.

Cinderella

One day, I will meet the prince. I will, I will, I will!

Narrator

Just then, there was a puff of smoke.

Cinderella

Who are you?

Narrator

It was Cinderella's fairy godmother. She asked Cinderella why she looked so sad.

Cinderella

The king wants all the girls in the land to meet the prince, but I can't go to the ball like this.

Narrator

So the fairy godmother waved her magic wand, and *poof* . . . Cinderella had a pink silk dress and fine glass slippers.

Cinderella

Wow! Look at me! Thank you, fairy godmother. Can I go to meet the prince now?

Narrator

The fairy godmother told Cinderella that she had to leave the ball before the clock struck 12:00. She told her to

Narrator

say some magic words, and Cinderella did.

Cinderella

One and two and three and four—I am at the castle door!

Narrator

Poof! Cinderella stepped into the castle. The prince looked at Cinderella, and Cinderella looked at the prince.

Stepsister

Who is that girl?

Stepmother

And where did she get such a fine pink dress?

Prince

Oh, my! Who is that girl? I will ask her to dance with me.

Narrator

The prince and Cinderella danced together all night long. Then, the clock started to chime. It was 12:00.

Cinderella

Oh, no, I have to go!

Prince

Please don't go! Please stay with me.

Cinderella

No, no! I have to go!

Narrator

Cinderella ran down the steps, but she lost one of her glass slippers.

Prince

I have to find the girl who lost this slipper. I want her to be my wife!

Narrator

The next day, the prince went to every house in the land.

Prince

I must find the girl who lost this slipper!

Narrator

Finally, the prince knocked on the door of Cinderella's house.

Stepsister

Oh, my, the prince is here!

Prince

Good day. I am the prince.
I am here to find the girl who
lost this glass slipper.

Stepsister

**That is MY glass slipper!
It will fit me. You will see!**

Narrator

So the prince tried to put the
slipper on her very big foot.

Stepmother

Oh, no! Let me help! You have
to get your foot into that
slipper!

Cinderella

May I try the glass slipper on my foot?

Prince

Who are you?

Stepsister

That is Cinderella. She just cleans the house!

Stepmother

Go away, Cinderella. Go to your room!

Prince

No. Please stay and try the slipper on your foot.

13

Narrator

So the prince got on his knees and slid the slipper onto Cinderella's foot.

Prince

It fits! You are the girl from the ball!

Stepsister

Oh, Mother, she was the girl who danced with the prince!

Stepmother

NOOOOOOOOOOOO! This cannot be true!

Prince

Cinderella

Narrator

Will you come to the castle and be my wife?

Yes, I will!

And from that time on, Cinderella and the prince lived happily ever after . . . and the mean stepmother and stepsister had to clean and scrub the house all by themselves!

Cinderella

THE PLAY

FEATURING:

The Prince

ALSO STARRING:

Stepmother
Stepsister
Cinderella
Narrator

Adapted by Nora Gaydos
Illustrated by Barbara Vagnozzi

Narrator

Once upon a time, there lived a nice girl named Cinderella. She lived with her mean stepmother and her mean stepsister.

Stepmother

Make the beds and mop the floors, Cinderella!

Stepsister

Scrub the tub and clean the plates, Cinderella!

1

Narrator

All day and night, Cinderella had to clean and mop and scrub the house. But she did it with a smile on her face.

Cinderella

One day, I will leave this house, and I will be happy all the time.

Narrator

Knock, knock, knock. A man was at the door with a note.

Stepmother

Look! The king wants all the girls in the land to come to a ball at the castle.

Stepsister

And the prince will pick one girl to be his wife! Oh, Mother, it just has to be me!

Cinderella

Or maybe it will be me! Yes, yes! I need to make a dress—and fast.

Stepmother

Stop, Cinderella! You will not go to the ball until you do all of your jobs.

Cinderella

But I just cleaned the whole house!

Stepsister

Well, now you need to fix my dress, brush my hair, shine my shoes, and clean the house . . . again!

Narrator

After doing all of her jobs, Cinderella had no time to make a dress for herself.

Stepmother

It is time for the ball, Cinderella. Too bad you have to stay home.

Stepsister

How sad for Cinderella. She will not get to meet the prince.

Cinderella

One day, I will meet the prince. I will, I will, I will!

Narrator

Just then, there was a puff of smoke.

Cinderella

Who are you?

Narrator

It was Cinderella's fairy godmother. She asked Cinderella why she looked so sad.

Cinderella

The king wants all the girls in the land to meet the prince, but I can't go to the ball like this.

So the fairy godmother waved her magic wand, and *poof* . . . Cinderella had a pink silk dress and fine glass slippers.

Wow! Look at me! Thank you, fairy godmother. Can I go to meet the prince now?

The fairy godmother told Cinderella that she had to leave the ball before the clock struck 12:00. She told her to

Narrator

say some magic words, and Cinderella did.

Cinderella

One and two and three and four—I am at the castle door!

Narrator

Poof! Cinderella stepped into the castle. The prince looked at Cinderella, and Cinderella looked at the prince.

Stepsister

Who is that girl?

Stepmother

And where did she get such a fine pink dress?

Prince

Oh, my! Who is that girl? I will ask her to dance with me.

Narrator

The prince and Cinderella danced together all night long. Then, the clock started to chime. It was 12:00.

Cinderella

Oh, no, I have to go!

Prince

Please don't go! Please stay with me.

Cinderella

No, no! I have to go!

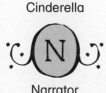

Narrator

Cinderella ran down the steps, but she lost one of her glass slippers.

Prince

I have to find the girl who lost this slipper. I want her to be my wife!

Narrator

The next day, the prince went to every house in the land.

Prince

I must find the girl who lost this slipper!

Narrator

Finally, the prince knocked on the door of Cinderella's house.

Stepsister

Oh, my, the prince is here!

Prince

Good day. I am the prince. I am here to find the girl who lost this glass slipper.

Stepsister

That is MY glass slipper! It will fit me. You will see!

Narrator

So the prince tried to put the slipper on her very big foot.

Stepmother

Oh, no! Let me help! You have to get your foot into that slipper!

Cinderella

May I try the glass slipper on my foot?

Prince

Who are you?

Stepsister

That is Cinderella. She just cleans the house!

Stepmother

Go away, Cinderella. Go to your room!

Prince

No. Please stay and try the slipper on your foot.

Narrator

So the prince got on his knees and slid the slipper onto Cinderella's foot.

Prince

It fits! You are the girl from the ball!

Stepsister

Oh, Mother, she was the girl who danced with the prince!

Stepmother

NOOOOOOOOOOOO! This cannot be true!

Prince

Will you come to the castle and be my wife?

Cinderella

Yes, I will!

Narrator

And from that time on, Cinderella and the prince lived happily ever after . . . and the mean stepmother and stepsister had to clean and scrub the house all by themselves!

Cinderella

THE STORY

Adapted by Nora Gaydos • Illustrated by Barbara Vagnozzi

Once upon a time, there lived a nice girl named Cinderella. She lived with her mean stepmother and her mean stepsister.

They made Cinderella clean the house all day and all night. But Cinderella always had a smile on her face.

One day, a man came to the door with a note. It said: "Come to a ball to meet the prince. He must find a wife."

"Oh, Mother! The prince HAS to pick me," said the mean stepsister.

"I hope that I can meet the prince, too," said Cinderella. "I will hurry and make a fine dress for myself."

But Cinderella's mean stepmother and stepsister laughed and laughed. They gave her a long list of jobs to do.

They told Cinderella that she could not go to the ball until she did everything on the list.

That night, Cinderella was still cleaning the house. She had no time to make herself a dress.

"Goodbye, Cinderella," said the mean stepmother.

"Too bad you will not get to meet the prince," said the mean stepsister.

Cinderella sat down in her dress of rags. She began to cry. Just then, there was a puff of smoke.

"I am your fairy godmother," said the woman. "Why do you look so sad?"

"The king wants all the girls in the land to meet the prince tonight, but I did not have time to make a dress for the ball," said Cinderella.

"I will help you," said the fairy godmother. And with a wave of her magic wand, she gave Cinderella a pink silk dress and fine glass slippers.

"Thank you, fairy godmother!" cried Cinderella. "Now I can meet the prince!"

Before Cinderella left for the ball, the fairy godmother had one warning:

"You must leave the ball before the clock strikes 12:00," she said. "At 12:00, the magic will fade, and your silk dress will turn back into rags."

Cinderella agreed. Then, the fairy godmother told Cinderella to spin around and say: "One and two and three and four . . . I am at the castle door."

And with a wave of the fairy godmother's hand, Cinderella was at the castle.

When Cinderella stepped inside, the prince saw her right away. They stared at each other. Then, he asked her to dance!

All night long, they danced together. Everyone wondered who this girl was . . . especially the mean stepmother and stepsister.

But then, the clock struck 12:00! Cinderella had to leave! She ran from the prince and down the castle steps. As she ran, one of her glass slippers fell off.

The prince found the slipper. "Now we must find the girl who lost this slipper," the prince told his father. "This is the girl who will be my wife!"

The next day, the prince took the glass slipper to every house in the land. But the prince had no luck. He could not find the girl whose foot fit inside the slipper.

Meanwhile, Cinderella was back to cleaning, scrubbing, and sweeping the house. But she still had a smile on her face.

She thought about the ball, and she hoped that she would see the prince again soon.

Just then, there was a knock at the door. It was the prince! He wanted all the girls in the house to try on the glass slipper.

"I will try it on," said the mean stepsister. "I know that slipper will fit on my foot!"

The stepsister grabbed the slipper and tried to get her big foot into it. But her foot was much too big!

The mean stepmother saw Cinderella peeking into the room. She tried to push her away, but the prince saw her.

"May I try the slipper on, too?" asked Cinderella.

"Yes," said the prince. He slid the slipper onto Cinderella's foot. It was a perfect fit! The mean stepmother and stepsister were very mad.

The prince took Cinderella by the hand. "You are the girl from the ball! Will you be my wife?"

"Oh, yes," she said. Cinderella was very, very happy.

From that moment on, the mean stepmother and stepsister had to clean the house all by themselves.

And Cinderella and the prince lived happily ever after.

THESE SIMPLE IDEAS
CAN HELP MAKE YOUR PLAY A HIT!

1 Make props to use in the play. You can either make your props using construction paper and crayons or markers, or you can use items from around the house. Some ideas for props: a mop, a dust pan, a fancy mirror, a clock, or fancy shoes.

2 Design scenery or backgrounds for the play using large chart paper or poster board and crayons or markers. Use the story as your guide, but here are some set ideas: inside the stepmother's house, the ball and dance floor, or outside the castle.

3 Along with the masks, use clothing you own to make costumes. Some costume ideas: a dress of rags for Cinderella, a gown for Cinderella, formal attire for the narrator, or a fancy suit and crown for the prince. You can also embellish the girls' costumes with jewelry, wigs, and high heels.

4 Create new characters! If you have more people that want to join in, add some lines to the play yourself! You can invent lines for the fairy godmother. You can make up another evil stepsister. Maybe the fairy godmother has helpers!

ENRICHING THE ACTING EXPERIENCE

Challenge kids to try these ideas while performing the play:

- Use expression and intonation to bring the play to life! For example: Give Cinderella a sweet and gentle voice or give the narrator a proper British accent.

- Memorize the lines! Suggest that kids try to remember a few lines at a time. Soon, they will be performing the play without using the book. This will free up their hands to allow them to add gesture and action.

- Videotape the play as it's performed. Kids will feel like real movie stars, and they will learn a lot by watching their performances afterward!

- Try performing the play as a puppet show. Use brown paper lunch bags to create puppets representing each of the characters. Then, go behind a couch with your books and put on the play using the puppets.

- Add background sound effects at different points throughout the play! This will create emotion and build suspense. For example: Create a sound effect for the mop on the floor, knock on something when someone comes to the door of the stepmother's house, make a sound for the puff of smoke when the fairy godmother enters, or you can even play music during the ball when Cinderella and the prince are dancing!

GOING BEYOND · MAKING CONNECTIONS

Not every kid learns the same way. Using alternative methods to introduce the play is a great way to get different kids excited about reading. For example, have your child or student make a:

- **READING CONNECTION:** Read other versions of *Cinderella*. Compare and contrast the different versions. Try to find the differences between the versions that your child or student just read.

- **WRITING CONNECTION:** Write a letter to one of the characters in the book to tell why he or she liked or disliked the character. The child or student can also tell the character what he or she thought the character should have done differently.

- **ART CONNECTION:** Design a ball gown for Cinderella! Make it out of paper or fabric, and decorate it with costume jewelry.

- **MATH CONNECTION:** Cinderella has to leave the ball at midnight. Create a clock using paper and a paper fastener. Cut out arrows to make movable hour and minute hands. Then, practice telling time with your handmade clock!

- **RHYMING CONNECTION:** Make a list of words that rhyme with the following: mop, king, ball, clock, wife, or any other words from the story!

- **HISTORY CONNECTION:** Some countries still have kings, queens, princes, and princesses. Use the public library or computer to research which countries have royalty and who these kings, queens, princes, and princesses are.

Cinderella
THE PLAY

FEATURING:

The Narrator

ALSO STARRING:

Cinderella
Stepmother
Stepsister
Prince

Adapted by Nora Gaydos
Illustrated by Barbara Vagnozzi

Narrator

Once upon a time, there lived a nice girl named Cinderella. She lived with her mean stepmother and her mean stepsister.

Stepmother

Make the beds and mop the floors, Cinderella!

Stepsister

Scrub the tub and clean the plates, Cinderella!

Narrator

All day and night, Cinderella had to clean and mop and scrub the house. But she did it with a smile on her face.

Cinderella

One day, I will leave this house, and I will be happy all the time.

Narrator

Knock, knock, knock. A man was at the door with a note.

Stepmother

Look! The king wants all the girls in the land to come to a ball at the castle.

Stepsister

And the prince will pick one girl to be his wife! Oh, Mother, it just has to be me!

Cinderella

Or maybe it will be me! Yes, yes! I need to make a dress— and fast.

Stepmother

Stop, Cinderella! You will not go to the ball until you do all of your jobs.

Cinderella

But I just cleaned the whole house!

Stepsister

Well, now you need to fix my dress, brush my hair, shine my shoes, and clean the house . . . again!

4

Narrator

After doing all of her jobs, Cinderella had no time to make a dress for herself.

Stepmother

It is time for the ball, Cinderella. Too bad you have to stay home.

Stepsister

How sad for Cinderella. She will not get to meet the prince.

Cinderella

One day, I will meet the prince. I will, I will, I will!

Narrator

Just then, there was a puff of smoke.

Cinderella

Who are you?

Narrator

It was Cinderella's fairy godmother. She asked Cinderella why she looked so sad.

Cinderella

The king wants all the girls in the land to meet the prince, but I can't go to the ball like this.

6

Narrator

So the fairy godmother waved her magic wand, and *poof* . . . Cinderella had a pink silk dress and fine glass slippers.

Cinderella

Wow! Look at me! Thank you, fairy godmother. Can I go to meet the prince now?

Narrator

The fairy godmother told Cinderella that she had to leave the ball before the

Narrator

clock struck 12:00. She told her to say some magic words, and Cinderella did.

Cinderella

One and two and three and four—I am at the castle door!

Narrator

***Poof!* Cinderella stepped into the castle. The prince looked at Cinderella, and Cinderella looked at the prince.**

Stepsister

Who is that girl?

Stepmother

And where did she get such a fine pink dress?

Prince

Oh, my! Who is that girl? I will ask her to dance with me.

Narrator

The prince and Cinderella danced together all night long. Then, the clock started to chime. It was 12:00.

Cinderella

Oh, no, I have to go!

Prince

Please don't go! Please stay with me.

Cinderella

No, no! I have to go!

Narrator

Cinderella ran down the steps, but she lost one of her glass slippers.

Prince

I have to find the girl who lost this slipper. I want her to be my wife!

Narrator

The next day, the prince went to every house in the land.

Prince

I must find the girl who lost this slipper!

Narrator

Finally, the prince knocked on the door of Cinderella's house.

Stepsister

Oh, my, the prince is here!

Prince

Good day. I am the prince.
I am here to find the girl who
lost this glass slipper.

Stepsister

That is MY glass slipper! It will
fit me. You will see!

Narrator

**So the prince tried to put the
slipper on her very big foot.**

Stepmother

Oh, no! Let me help! You have
to get your foot into that
slipper!

Cinderella

May I try the glass slipper on my foot?

Prince

Who are you?

Stepsister

That is Cinderella. She just cleans the house!

Stepmother

Go away, Cinderella. Go to your room!

Prince

No. Please stay and try the slipper on your foot.

13

Narrator

So the prince got on his knees and slid the slipper onto Cinderella's foot.

Prince

It fits! You are the girl from the ball!

Stepsister

Oh, Mother, she was the girl who danced with the prince!

Stepmother

NOOOOOOOOOOOO! This cannot be true!

Prince

Will you come to the castle and be my wife?

Cinderella

Yes, I will!

Narrator

And from that time on, Cinderella and the prince lived happily ever after . . . and the mean stepmother and stepsister had to clean and scrub the house all by themselves!

Cinderella

THE PLAY

FEATURING:

Cinderella

ALSO STARRING:

Stepmother
Stepsister
Prince
Narrator

Adapted by Nora Gaydos
Illustrated by Barbara Vagnozzi

Narrator

Once upon a time, there lived a nice girl named Cinderella. She lived with her mean stepmother and her mean stepsister.

Stepmother

Make the beds and mop the floors, Cinderella!

Stepsister

Scrub the tub and clean the plates, Cinderella!

Narrator

All day and night, Cinderella had to clean and mop and scrub the house. But she did it with a smile on her face.

Cinderella

One day, I will leave this house, and I will be happy all the time.

Narrator

Knock, knock, knock. A man was at the door with a note.

Stepmother

Look! The king wants all the girls in the land to come to a ball at the castle.

Stepsister

And the prince will pick one girl to be his wife! Oh, Mother, it just has to be me!

Cinderella

Or maybe it will be me! Yes, yes! I need to make a dress—and fast.

Stepmother

Stop, Cinderella! You will not go to the ball until you do all of your jobs.

Cinderella

But I just cleaned the whole house!

Stepsister

Well, now you need to fix my dress, brush my hair, shine my shoes, and clean the house . . . again!

Narrator

After doing all of her jobs, Cinderella had no time to make a dress for herself.

Stepmother

It is time for the ball, Cinderella. Too bad you have to stay home.

Stepsister

How sad for Cinderella. She will not get to meet the prince.

Cinderella

One day, I will meet the prince. I will, I will, I will!

Narrator

Just then, there was a puff of smoke.

Cinderella

Who are you?

Narrator

It was Cinderella's fairy godmother. She asked Cinderella why she looked so sad.

Cinderella

The king wants all the girls in the land to meet the prince, but I can't go to the ball like this.

Narrator

So the fairy godmother waved her magic wand, and *poof* . . . Cinderella had a pink silk dress and fine glass slippers.

Cinderella

You can add your tiara to your mask now!

Wow! Look at me! Thank you, fairy godmother. Can I go to meet the prince now?

Narrator

The fairy godmother told Cinderella that she had to leave the ball before the clock struck 12:00. She told her to

Narrator

say some magic words, and Cinderella did.

Cinderella

One and two and three and four—I am at the castle door!

Narrator

Poof! Cinderella stepped into the castle. The prince looked at Cinderella, and Cinderella looked at the prince.

Stepsister

Who is that girl?

Stepmother

And where did she get such a fine pink dress?

Prince

Oh, my! Who is that girl? I will ask her to dance with me.

Narrator

The prince and Cinderella danced together all night long. Then, the clock started to chime. It was 12:00.

Cinderella

Oh, no, I have to go!

Prince

Please don't go! Please stay with me.

Cinderella

No, no! I have to go!

Narrator

Cinderella ran down the steps, but she lost one of her glass slippers.

Prince

I have to find the girl who lost this slipper. I want her to be my wife!

Narrator

The next day, the prince went to every house in the land.

Prince

I must find the girl who lost this slipper!

Narrator

Finally, the prince knocked on the door of Cinderella's house.

Stepsister

Oh, my, the prince is here!

Prince

Good day. I am the prince.
I am here to find the girl who
lost this glass slipper.

Stepsister

That is MY glass slipper! It will
fit me. You will see!

Narrator

So the prince tried to put the
slipper on her very big foot.

Stepmother

Oh, no! Let me help! You have
to get your foot into that
slipper!

Cinderella

May I try the glass slipper on my foot?

Prince

Who are you?

Stepsister

That is Cinderella. She just cleans the house!

Stepmother

Go away, Cinderella. Go to your room!

Prince

No. Please stay and try the slipper on your foot.

Narrator

So the prince got on his knees and slid the slipper onto Cinderella's foot.

Prince

It fits! You are the girl from the ball!

Stepsister

Oh, Mother, she was the girl who danced with the prince!

Stepmother

NOOOOOOOOOOOO! This cannot be true!

Prince

Will you come to the castle and be my wife?

Cinderella

Yes, I will!

Narrator

And from that time on, Cinderella and the prince lived happily ever after . . . and the mean stepmother and stepsister had to clean and scrub the house all by themselves!